Clifford™
TUMMY TROUBLE

Adapted by Josephine Page
Illustrated by Ken Edwards

◼SCHOLASTIC

From the television script
"Tummy Trouble" by Lois Becker and Mark Stratton

"Today you will do a trick for your treat,"
Emily Elizabeth said to Clifford.

She held up a treat for Clifford to sniff.
"Down, Clifford," she said.
Clifford lay down.

Then he sat up, opened his mouth,
and waited for his treat.

Emily Elizabeth tossed the treat into Clifford's mouth.
"Good boy," she said. "Roll over."

Clifford rolled over.
He rolled and rolled and rolled.

Then he sat up, opened his mouth, and waited for his treat.

Cleo and T-Bone walked by.
"Why are you sitting like that?" Cleo asked.

"I'm waiting for Emily Elizabeth to give me a treat," Clifford said. "I did a trick for her."

"I saw Emily Elizabeth in her mother's car,"
said T-Bone. "They drove away."

"I will give you a treat," said Cleo.
Cleo gave Clifford a treat.

She gave T-Bone a treat.
And she gave herself a treat.
"You have to do a trick for your treat,"
Clifford said.

T-Bone stood on his hind legs.
"That was very clever," Cleo said.

She tossed a second treat to T-Bone.
"That was a good throw," T-Bone said.

Cleo gave herself a treat for her good throw.

"You'll be sick if you eat too many treats,"
Clifford said.

"Thank you for worrying about me," said Cleo.
"That was very kind. You should get
another treat."

T-Bone chased his tail.
Cleo tossed him a treat and gave herself a treat
for her good throw.

Clifford walked on his front paws.
Everyone got a treat for that.

Clifford and T-Bone did many more tricks.
Cleo tossed more treats.

Until the whole box of treats was empty!

"Don't worry," said Cleo. "We still have two
boxes full of treats."

"My tummy hurts," said T-Bone.
"Mine hurts, too," said Clifford.

"You're probably hungry," said Cleo. "Have some more treats."

Soon two boxes of treats were empty.
Then three boxes of treats were empty.

T-Bone lay on his back.

"I'm full," said Cleo, who had a very big tummy.

"Me, too," said T-Bone, who had an even bigger tummy.

"Me, three," said Clifford. He had the biggest tummy of all.

Emily Elizabeth came back with treats for Clifford and his friends.
She saw the three empty boxes.

She saw the three sick dogs.

"Poor doggies," she said. "You shouldn't have eaten all those treats.

But everyone makes mistakes sometimes – even the biggest, reddest, best dog in the world. I love you, Clifford."

Other Clifford Storybooks:

The Big Leaf Pile
The Runaway Rabbit
The Show-and-Tell Surprise

Scholastic Children's Books
Commonwealth House, 1-19 New Oxford Street, London WC1A 1NU
A division of Scholastic Ltd
London ~ New York ~ Toronto ~ Sydney ~ Auckland ~ Mexico City ~ New Delhi ~ Hong Kong

First published in the USA by Scholastic Inc., 2000
This edition published in the UK by Scholastic Ltd, 2002

ISBN 0 439 98148 4

1 2 3 4 5 6 7 8 9 10 Printed in Italy by Amadeus S.p.A. – Rome